SHONEN JUMP'S

Yu-Gi-Oh! GX

Adapted by Tracey West

RESCUE DUEL

SCHOLASTIC INC.

| New York | Toronto | London | Auckland | Sydney |
| Mexico City | New Delhi | Hong Kong | Buenos Aires |

ISBN-13: 978-0-439-88840-0
ISBN-10: 0-439-88840-9

© 1996 Kazuki Takahashi
© 2004 NAS•TV TOKYO

Published by Scholastic Inc.
SCHOLASTIC and associated logos are trademarks and/or registered trademarks of Scholastic Inc.

12 11 10 9 8 7 6 5 4 3 2 1   7 8 9 10 11/0

Printed in the U.S.A.
First printing, January 2007

"Chazz! Chazz!" Jaden Yuki called out.

He and his friend Syrus walked through the woods on Academy Island.

They were looking for Chazz Princeton, a student missing from school.

Alexis, Jasmine, and Mindy helped, too. "We're going to come with you," Alexis said. "Chazz is an Obelisk Blue. And we take care of our own!"

They walked and walked. Then Alexis saw something in the trees.

She pointed. "Look there! Something's moving!"

They all walked ahead, when suddenly . . .

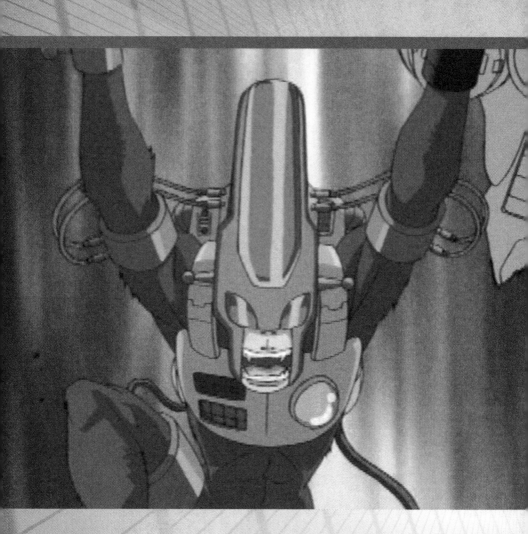

Something jumped out of the bushes at them!

It grabbed Jasmine and ran off.

"What's that thing?" Syrus asked.

"Help!" Jasmine screamed.

They ran after the sound. Some kind of monkey had Jasmine! It swung from tree to tree. Then it stopped at a steep cliff. Jasmine held on tightly to a tree branch.

Three men ran out of the trees. One of them pointed a weapon at the monkey.

"Fire when ready!" a tall man in dark glasses shouted.

"Hey, that monkey has a Duel Disk on!" Jaden cried.

"That's no regular monkey," the smallest man said. "His name is Wheeler. He's a trained duelist!"

The tall man frowned. "Sir . . ."

"Oh, yes," the professor said. "Forgot. Top Secret."

Jaden had an idea.

"Let me duel him!" he said. "I bet if I beat this monkey, he will hand over Jasmine." He looked at Wheeler. "Ready to get your game on?"

Jaden and Wheeler turned on their Duel Disks.

"Let's duel!" Jaden cried.

"Duel!" came a computer voice from the monkey.

"His helmet reads his mind and talks for him," the professor explained.

Jaden and Wheeler started with 4000 life points each.

Jaden drew five cards. He put one on the field.

"Go, Elemental Hero Sparkman!" he cried.

The blue and gold hero stood in front of Jaden.

"My turn!" Wheeler cried. "Berserk Gorilla! Attack Sparkman! Attack!"

The hairy beast had 2000 attack points. It pounded Sparkman with a huge fist. The hero exploded, and Jaden's life points dropped to 3600.

"Jaden's losing his cool," Alexis said. "I mean, he is getting beat by a monkey!"

"Gimme a break!" Jaden cried. "The duel just started!"

ATK 2100

Jaden used Polymerization to make Elemental Hero Flame Wingman.

"Go, Infernal Rage!" Jaden yelled.

Flame Wingman threw a fire ball at Berserk Gorilla.

Blam! The beast vanished from the field. Wheeler's life points dropped to 3900.

"I'm not done yet," Jaden said. "Next I'll use Flame Wingman's superpower. You lose life points equal to what your destroyed monster's attack points were!"

Wheeler cried out as his life points fell 2000 points—all the way down to 1900!

Wheeler fell to his knees.

"Are you calling it quits already?" Jaden asked.

"Oh, please," said the professor. "Back in the lab, if he made the same mistake twice, he would be harshly punished. He won't give up. He'll just get better!"

Jaden felt sorry for Wheeler. The lab sounded like an awful place.

Wheeler got back on his feet. "I summon Acrobat Monkey!" he cried.

A monkey in silver armor appeared on the field.

"Next, I play my facedown. Trap! Trap!" Wheeler yelled.

Wheeler turned over the card. "DNA Surgery!"

Jaden knew that card. It could change all monsters on the field to whatever type of monster Wheeler wanted.

"I choose Beast-type! Beast-type!" Wheeler screamed.

Acrobat Monkey got bigger, with sharp teeth. Wingman transformed into a dragonlike beast with a long tail.

"I play Wild Nature's Release!" Wheeler cried.

Acrobat Monkey life points jumped up to 2800.

"Acrobat Monkey, attack!" Wheeler yelled.

The beast charged across the field. It pounded Wingman with its fists. Wingman shattered into pieces, and Jaden's life points dropped down to 2900.

But then Acrobat Monkey exploded, too!
"When Wild Nature's Release is used
on a monster, that monster is destroyed at
the end of the turn," Alexis explained.
    Jaden drew another card. He was not
going to let some monkey beat him.

Then he heard a noise. He turned to see a big group of monkeys behind a rock. The monkeys looked at Wheeler sadly.

Jaden understood. "That's why you were trying to escape, isn't it? To get back to your family!"

Wheeler jumped up and down. "Must win! Miss family!"

"Well, I need to get Jasmine back," Jaden said. "So unless you let her go, I have to beat you!"

Jaden summoned Elemental Hero Clayman. Thanks to DNA Surgery, the big hero transformed into a huge wolf. He had 800 attack points.

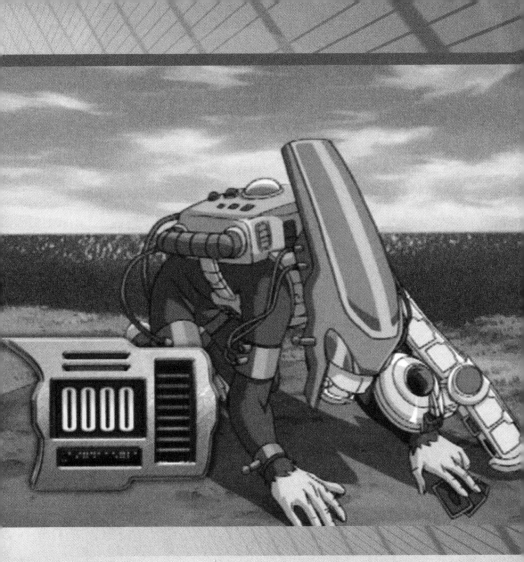

Then Jaden played another card. "Courageous Charge!" Jaden cried. He paid 1000 life points. But it gave Clayman more power.

Clayman attacked Wheeler directly. "Eeeeeeeeeek!" Wheeler screamed as his life points fell to 0.

"Fair's fair," Jaden said. "Time you let Jasmine go."

Wheeler nodded sadly. He gently picked up Jasmine and put her on the ground.

The men moved to grab Wheeler. But Jaden stood in front of them.

"He doesn't belong with you," Jaden said. "He belongs out here with his family, got it?"

But the men pushed Jaden aside. They threw a net on Wheeler.

The professor looked at the other monkeys. "Your friend won't miss his family," he said. "I'm taking them all!"

"We won't let you take them back to the lab!" Syrus cried.

The professor just laughed. "You think your threats scare me?"

Suddenly, a cat jumped out of nowhere. It attacked the men.

Professor Banner stepped out of the woods. "Tsk-tsk, Pharaoh," he said. "Naughty kitty."

The men knew not to mess with Professor Banner. They ran away—and left the monkeys alone.

Wheeler took off his helmet—but he
kept his Duel Disk. He ran to his family.
"Let's duel again sometime!" Jaden
called out, waving good-bye.

Professor Banner took the kids to the boat docks.

"I wanted to tell you that Chazz is okay," he explained. "But there's some bad news as well. He left on his family's boat."

"That's a shame," Jaden said. He looked out over the water. "After all, good rivals are hard to find!"